MAKING THE GRADE ·

EASY POPULAR PIECES FOR YOUNG CLARINETTISTS SELECTED AND ARRANGED BY JERRY LANNING

GW00418922

Exclusive Distributors:
Music Sales Limited
Newmarket Road, Bury St. Edmunds, Suffolk IP33 3YB.
This book © copyright 1992 Chester Music.
ISBN 0-7119-2942-4
Order No. CH60056
Cover designed by Pemberton and Whitefoord
Typeset by Pemberton and Whitefoord
Printed in the United Kingdom by
Caligraving Limited, Thetford, Norfolk.

Chester Music

(A division of Music Sales Limited)
8/9 Frith Street, London W1V 5TZ.

INTRODUCTION

This collection of 21 popular tunes has been carefully arranged and graded to provide attractive teaching repertoire for young clarinettists. The familiarity of the material will stimulate pupils' enthusiasm and encourage their practice.

The technical demands of the solo part increase progressively up to the standard of Associated Board Grade 1. The piano accompaniments are simple yet effective and should be within the range of most pianists.

Breath marks are given throughout, showing the most musically desirable places to take a breath. Students may also need to take additional breaths when learning a piece or practising at a slower tempo, and suitable opportunities are indicated by breath marks in brackets.

LOVE ME TENDER

Words & Music by Elvis Presley & Vera Matson.

Play the phrases smoothly, and keep a steady tempo.
Try to breath only at the places marked with a tick.

BANKS OF THE OHIO

Traditional.

Look out for the rests at the beginning of bars 2, 4, 6, 8 and 12.

Take a breath on the first beat and play on the second.

Gently

SUPERCALIFRAGILISTICEXPIALIDOCIOUS

Words & Music by Richard M. Sherman & Robert B. Sherman.

Tongue the repeated Ds clearly, but don't make them staccato.

ON CHRISTMAS NIGHT

Traditional.

Although the notes are quite easy, this piece needs good breath control to sound effective.
Observe the breath marks carefully.

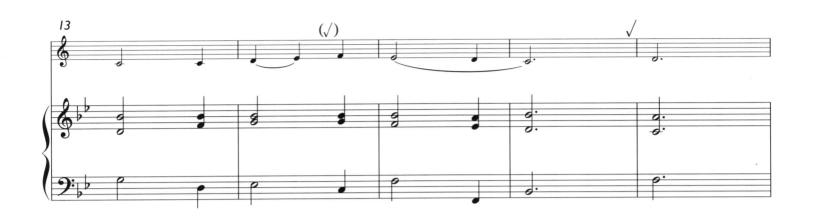

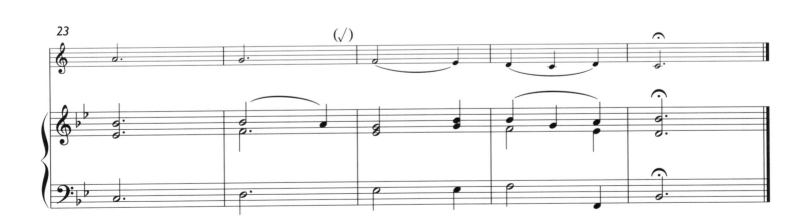

BLOWIN' IN THE WIND

Words & Music by Bob Dylan.

Notice how the first four-bar phrase is repeated five times with slight variations,
and 'answered' by the final eight bars.

Flowing

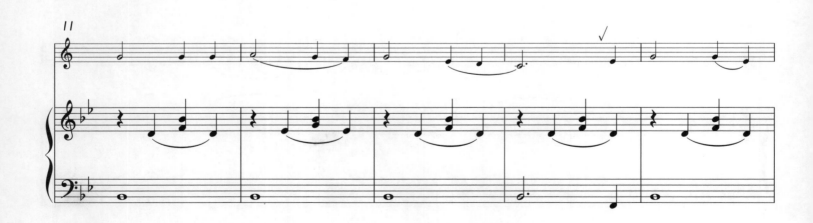

SOMETIMES WHEN WE TOUCH

Words & Music by Dan Hill & Barry Mann.

Although there are a number of repeated notes here,
this piece should generally sound smooth and sustained.

* easier alternative.

WE ALL STAND TOGETHER

Words & Music by Paul McCartney.

Play bars 9 to 12 in one breath if you can.

I'D LIKE TO TEACH THE WORLD TO SING

Words & Music by Roger Cook, Roger Greenaway, Billy Backer & Billy Davis.

In bar 4 you will need to take a very quick breath after the third beat

so as not to be late playing the C on the fourth beat.

Moderately bright

ODE TO JOY (THEME FROM THE 9TH SYMPHONY)

Composed by Ludwig Van Beethoven.

This is the main theme from one of Beethoven's biggest works.
It needs a good, strong sound.

TALES OF THE UNEXPECTED (THEME FROM)

Composed by Ron Grainer.

This is the theme from the popular TV series.
Notice the clever mixture of three-, four- and five-bar phrases which give it a haunting quality.

JINGLE BELLS

Traditional.

Make the staccato notes in bar 3 contrast with the repeated notes in bar 7.

The slurred sixths in the verse (bar 19 etc.) will need some special practice.

MORNING HAS BROKEN

Music Traditional.

Practise the scale and arpeggio of G major (slurred, not tongued) before you tackle this one.

Notice the different rhythms in bars 13 and 25.

CHIM CHIM CHER-EE

Words & Music by Richard M. Sherman & Robert B. Sherman.

Accent the first beat and play the rest of the bar quite lightly, to give a real one-in-a-bar feel.

LITTLE BROWN JUG

Traditional.

Make sure all the quavers are really even.

Practise bar 11 until you can tongue the semiquavers clearly.

SCARBOROUGH FAIR

Traditional.

Practise each four-bar phrase separately, trying not to take a breath in the middle of it.

AMAZING GRACE

Traditional.

You will need to keep a steady tempo. If you find the rhythm difficult,
try clapping it while you count the beats out loud.

Quite slowly

THIS OLE HOUSE

Words & Music by Stuart Hamblen.

Here's a lively American country and western song which will give you practice in repeated notes.
Accent the first beat in each bar slightly.

ONE DAY AT A TIME

Words & Music by Marijohn Wilkin & Kris Kristofferson.

This beautiful gospel song was a big hit a few years back.

Make sure you hold the tied notes for their full value.

HEY JUDE (1ST VERSION)

Words & Music by John Lennon & Paul McCartney.

If you find the rhythms in this Beatles song tricky, try the version opposite first,
where the note lengths have been doubled.

Quite slowly (in 4)

HEY JUDE (2ND VERSION)

Words & Music by John Lennon & Paul McCartney.

If you count four in a bar to begin with, you'll have no trouble with the rhythms.

When you are able to play up to speed (counting in two), go back to the first version.

Quite slowly (in 2)

COUNTRY GARDENS

Traditional.

This very popular folk tune was originally a morris dance.
Look out for the sudden *piano* in bar 12 (which echoes bar 11).

EASTENDERS

Composed by Leslie Osborne & Simon May.

Be careful not to rush the triplet crotchets, but give them a broad, slightly lazy feel.

6/98 (31088)